KV-511-033

This book belongs to:

_____

A catalogue record for this book is available from the British Library

Published by Ladybird Books Ltd
80 Strand, London, WC2R 0RL
A Penguin Company

2 4 6 8 10 9 7 5 3 1
© LADYBIRD BOOKS LTD MMIX
LADYBIRD and the device of a Ladybird are trademarks of Ladybird Books Ltd

ISBN: 978-140930-170-7

Printed in China

Five-minute Tales
Messiest Monster Ever

written by Rebecca Lim
illustrated by Caroline Freake

Fernando Makes a Mess

Fernando Monster lived in a big, monster house with his parents, Mr and Mrs Monster, and his sister, Betty Monster.

Fernando went to monster school, and he did his monster homework, and he played nicely with all the other little monsters. "What a good little monster you are!" said his mum, proudly.

One day, Fernando decided to do finger-painting. His neat and tidy sister, Betty, was doing her neat and tidy jigsaw. Fernando made a lovely squiggly picture. Splat! Whoops! Fernando knocked over the paint pots.

Then Fernando went to hang up his painting. Squish! Squelch! Fernando left a trail of squidgy red footprints on the floor. Fernando was quite a messy monster, wasn't he?

SQUISH!

SQUELCH!

But Fernando wasn't finished. He decided to do just one more finger-painting.
"I'm not going to just use my fingers, that's boring!" said Fernando, the messy monster.
So what else did Fernando use? His nose!

Now there was paint all over the floor…
and all over Fernando. What a mess!
"I'll just wash off this paint…" said Fernando.
And he found a lovely muddy puddle
outside to jump in.

Was Fernando messy enough by now?
No, he wasn't. One puddle jump is never
enough for a messy monster! Split! Splat!
Pretty soon, Fernando was covered in
paint and mud.

Fernando went squelch, squelch…
happily back into the kitchen. There never
was a messier little monster. Fernando just
couldn't help it!
"Oh, Fernando!" said his mum, smiling.
"You really are the messiest monster ever!"

A Visit to the Park

Fernando Monster was very excited. Daddy was taking him and his friends, Alfie and George, to the park. "Try not to let them get too messy today," said Mummy. "Yes, dear," said Daddy.

Fernando liked everything about Monster Park, but most of all he loved it after the rain, when lots of muddy puddles sprang up everywhere.

What was it Fernando liked so much about muddy puddles? He loved splashing and jumping in them.

"Now, we're trying not to get too messy today," said his dad.

"Yes, Daddy," said Fernando. He really tried to be a good little monster. And then Fernando rushed off to play. Daddy Monster sat down to read the newspaper.

What was the first thing the three monster friends did? Jump in the muddy puddles, of course!

"Yippee!" they yelled. They were soaking wet, but Daddy didn't notice.

"What about the sandpit next?" he said.

Fernando and his friends made a big sandcastle, and covered each other in the sand, and rolled about. What fun it was, being muddy and sandy monsters! Daddy was still reading his newspaper. "Time for a monster slide," he said, without looking up.

What do you think was waiting for the
three friends at the bottom of the slide?
A lovely, big, monster puddle to land in!
"Time to go home," said Daddy.
And then he noticed the muddy monsters.
"Hmm," said Daddy. But he was smiling.
He knew Fernando just couldn't help it.

SPLISH!

At home, Daddy was still smiling.

"One happy, messy little monster," he said.

Mummy laughed.

"Oh, Fernando!" she said. "You really are the messiest monster ever!"

"Yes," said Fernando proudly. "And this time it was all Daddy's idea!"

Fernando's Surprise

On Sundays, Mummy Monster took her little monsters to see their grandparents. "Have fun," she said and gave them a big hug.

Grandma and Grandpa's monster house was called Magnificent Manor. It had a big front door and seven chimneys! Grandma Monster even had a pet sheep, to keep the grass neat in the garden.

"I must try not to make a mess," said Fernando. Then he ran into the house and up the stairs, past a big vase of flowers and... what do you think happened next?

CRASH!

Crash! Oh dear! Fernando fell over.
He knocked over the vase. Flowers
flew everywhere. Water splashed on
the carpet. What a mess!

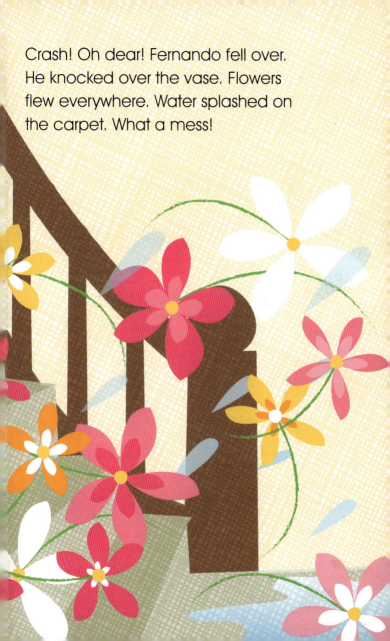

Crash! Smash! Oh dear! Fernando fell over again. He knocked over an umbrella stand. Umbrellas flew everywhere. What a terrible mess!

"Whoops!" said Fernando, the messy monster. He picked himself up. He turned around, and… Clatter! Boom! He knocked over a statue. One, two, three messes! "Never mind! Let's go and get the dustpan and brush," said Grandpa, kindly.

BOOM!

CLATTER!

CRUNCH!

Grandpa and Fernando walked into
the kitchen… and there was Grandma,
making ice cream with Betty. There was
ice cream everywhere! It was all over
the table and all over Grandma.
"Tee-hee!" said Grandma. "What a mess!"

As they ate their delicious ice creams,
Grandma said, "When I was little, I was
the messiest monster ever. Sometimes,
I still make a mess – I just can't help it!"
What a surprise! Fernando laughed.
He laughed so hard he fell forward…
and what do you think happened next?